the world's GREATEST underachiever

HankZipZer

**Hank Zipzer the World's
Greatest Underachiever series
by Henry Winkler and Lin Oliver**

The Crazy Classroom Cascade

The Crunchy Pickle Disaster

The Mutant Moth

The Lucky Monkey Socks

The Soggy School Trip

The Killer Chilli

The Parent-Teacher Trouble

The Best Worst Summer Ever

The Ping-Pong Wizard

The House of Halloween Horrors

Who Ordered This Baby? Definitely Not Me!

The Curtain Went Up, My Trousers Fell Down

A Tale of Two Tails

The Life of Me (Enter at Your Own Risk)

the world's GREATEST underachiever

HankZ!pZER

THE PIZZA PARTY AND
THE PLAGUE OF LOCUSTS

THEO BAKER

WALKER
ENTERTAINMENT

First published in Great Britain 2016 by Walker Entertainment,
an imprint of Walker Books Ltd, 87 Vauxhall Walk, London SE11 5HJ

Based on the television series "Hank Zipzer"
produced by Kindle Entertainment
in association with DHX Media Ltd.
Based on the screenplay *Camouflage*.
Reproductions © 2014 Hank Zipzer Productions Limited

2 4 6 8 10 9 7 5 3 1

Text © 2016 Walker Books Ltd
Cover by Walker Books Ltd

This book has been typeset in OpenDyslexic

Printed and bound in Great Britain by Clays Ltd, St Ives plc

British Library Cataloguing in Publication Data:
a catalogue record for this book is available from the British Library

ISBN 978-1-4063-6790-4

www.walker.co.uk

CHAPTER ONE

Do you ever wish that you had a superpower?

Me too. Ever since I can remember. The first one I ever really wanted was the ability to eat metal. Don't ask me why. I was only three, and for whatever reason, I thought my life would be perfect if I could just take little nibbles out of water faucets and car bumpers whenever I wanted. I even had dreams about devouring entire skyscrapers...

The next superpower I really wanted was the ability to smell fear. You know, like a dog. Somehow I got it in my head that if I could smell fear, then no one would ever bother me or yell at me again, and I could chase away burglars and everybody would pet me and call me "good boy" and give me biscuits, and I could take the biscuits to my special place in the hallway and—

I'm pretty sure I wanted that power because we'd just got a little puppy, called Cheerio. He was a dachshund, one of those tiny little sausage dogs with cute pointy noses. I never did get fear-sniffing powers, like Cheerio, but I *did* start trying to eat my food out of a bowl on the floor, and I *did* start trying to go to the toilet on the ... listen, I was four. OK? And soon after that infamous newspaper incident, my parents told me that Cheerio missed his old home, and had asked to go back to his farm in the countryside so he could be with Grandma Cheerio.

I've wanted all sorts of superpowers over

my twelve years here on planet Earth. Most of the powers have involved the ability to sniff out something, or to eat something that's not actually food. But the one I've always wanted more than anything else is the power to be invisible. I know what you're thinking – everybody wants that power. It's the most unoriginal power you could possibly want. Everybody wants to sneak around, and look through people's stuff, and maybe steal some precious jewels ... but that's not why I want it. You see, I do have something of a superpower: I always end up in mad situations.

Every time I look up, I'm in a mad situation.

I'm actually in one at this very moment. And I'd do anything for an invisibility cloak right now, and I mean anything. I'd even eat locusts.

I am on the floor, flat on my stomach, underneath Miss Adolf's desk. My nose is about six inches from Miss Adolf's feet, and a moment ago — while I was telling you about poor little Cheerio — Miss Adolf decided to kick off her shoes and get comfortable. Her feet smell like damp cheese and curry, and oh no, I feel a sneeze coming on. It's in my nose already. My face is starting to scrunch up. It's going to happen. And since I'll only have a few minutes to live after it's out, and since my invisibility cloak is once again on the blink, I might as well tell you how I got here.

It all started with World War I.

CHAPTER TWO

Three weeks earlier.

When Miss Adolf asked for a volunteer to try on a gas mask, an authentic one from World War I, there was no question that I was going to be that volunteer. It all happened so fast. I don't even think I raised my hand. One moment Miss Adolf was taking out the gas mask from her bag, the next moment I was at the front of the class, the thing pressed against my face, with Miss Adolf tightening the straps to skull-crushing levels.

"Too tight!" I gasped, to everyone's laughter.

"It's got to be air-tight. You don't want to inhale mustard gas, do you?"

"I want to get out of this thing!"

"Notice, class, how difficult it is to speak wearing one of these gas masks," Miss Adolf said, and yanked the strap tighter.

"You're crushing my ear!"

"We can no longer understand *anything* Hank has to say. All we can hear is a low, grunting sound." The class was loving it, laughing and pointing. "So you can imagine how difficult it was for soldiers to hear their comrades in the trenches, surrounded by machine-gun and artillery fire."

I was starting to get a little woozy. The goggles had steamed up from all my breathing, and the thing smelled like 100-year-old saliva, just like that spit valve in the music room's trombone, the one that has been used by generations of kids. "Can I barf in this thing?!"

"Henry looks and sounds more ant-eater than human, don't you think, pupils?"

Through the steamy eye holes I saw that Miss Adolf looked quite pleased with herself for that one. She did that thing where it looked like she was trying to smile, but with her face so used to frowning and glaring all the time, it looked less like she was enjoying herself and more like she'd just eaten a bit of tainted meat.

"You sure there's no mustard gas left in there?" my best friend Frankie asked.

Miss Adolf thought about it for a moment. "I'm *mostly* sure."

"If there's mustard gas in there," my other best friend Ashley said, "he could go temporarily blind, and get diarrhoea!" Ashley is, by the way, super interested in grisly medical stuff.

Miss Adolf sighed.

She unloosened the straps, and I threw

13

off the mask.

"Now Hank, what was it you were trying to say?"

"I'm blind, Miss Adolf!" I flailed my arms around. "I can't see. Let me touch your face! Oh, it's so dark in my world! So dark!"

For an instant, the class was laughing with me. But then Miss Adolf swooshed her fencing sword through the air and sliced the good feeling in two. She's really quick with that thing. Ninja quick. I don't even know where she pulled it out of. "Settle down. The Great War was no laughing matter! That's something you'll learn while working on your essay—"

Everyone groaned.

"Yes," she said. "Your history project is to write an essay on life in the trenches of World War I. Five pages, single-spaced. No illustrations, no emojis, no late papers accepted whatsoever. You will also give a presentation. The presentation will only account for twenty per cent of your final grade. So if you think you can get out of writing your paper with an art project or interpretive dance, think again. I'm looking at you, Henry."

CHAPTER THREE

Three weeks sounds like a long time, right?
   And it is.

   I had plenty of time to start reading
about Prussian political alliances from
1907, plenty of time for my eyes to get all
hazy, and my brain all bored. That's when I
noticed a whole box of brand new rubbers,
and since I had practically a thousand years
to read about Prussian political alliances
from 1907, I just started making a miniature
Prussian army out of rubbers instead. And
I did it properly too. Like with hand-drawn

faces and paperclip bayonets. It took me a while to find just the right item for the little helmets, and for a while there, I was pretty stuck. Then I decided to take down everything from my bulletin board and use those metal pushpins for little helmets. They were adorable and perfect. I had a smartly uniformed army all standing in formation, and plenty of time, so I made a scale-model replica of the Palace of Versailles out of mashed potato, and set it out in the sun to harden. When the Palace started to smell a bit dodgy, I still had plenty of time to plan and then launch a massive siege on the Palace of Stink with my Prussian army of rubbers.

And that leads us to now. Three weeks are now a memory. And other than learning that there were indeed trenches in World War I, I've got nothing. Strike that, I've got *less* than nothing, because three weeks ago I had a box of rubbers.

Well, looks like my brain has done it again. Come on brain, why do you keep doing this to me? Huh?

No answer?

You know, brain, I listened to you for three weeks. I gave you nothing but fun little distractions. Now I'm here, and you owe me. I'm going to count to three and you're going to tell me exactly what to do. Or how I can get out of doing it. I need a miracle here. OK, ready?

1 ... 2 ... 3!

Fine, brain, be that way. I'll do it myself. With no help from you.

I shook myself all over, tugged my hair, mushed my face, widened my eyes and let out one of my getting-down-to-business screams, which my downstairs neighbour, Ms DeLillo, just loves. Feeling better, focused and ready for action, I picked up the book and scanned the table of contents for trench warfare. *The Origins of the ... Otto*

Von Bismarck's Four-Pronged Gambit ... The Balkans and the rise of the ... Powder Keg Europe ... Doughnuts with Powdered Sugar ... Chocolate Ice Cream with...

I shut the book and wandered over to the kitchen. Time for a little snack. You know, a little brain food.

CHAPTER FOUR

Things were happening in the living room. Dad was packing his overnight bag, and Mum was sitting on the couch, nervously hunched over a book called *Taking Your Child to the Hospital*.

I was fine, by the way. It was my noxious little sister, Emily — she was the one with all the mutant germs. She was going to the hospital the next day to have her tonsils taken out. It would be a pretty minor little surgery, I guess, but she would get to miss two weeks of school. Two whole weeks!

Wait — something clicked in my brain...

"Um, Mum," I croaked in a whisper, and swallowed with great anguish. I made my eyes look sickly and sad too. "My throat is ... *gulp* ... it's not..."

"Make yourself some tea with honey, love," Mum said without looking up.

"But maybe I should ... *gulp* ... go to the hospital and get..."

"Your tonsils surgically removed?" my dad said.

"Yeah," I whispered.

"An unnecessary surgery?" my dad asked again, looking quite greenish all of a sudden. "You want doctors to reach into your mouth and cut out part of your body?"

Of course I did. For two weeks of no school, they could cut whatever useless part of my body they wanted. Tonsils, appendix, nipples, brain — it was all the same to me.

"I think I have to," I croaked. "My throat

... gulp ... it burns..."

"Not now, Hank," Mum said from her book. "Tomorrow is a complex day for your sister. I need to keep this space calm and supportive."

Nobody in my family believed my little acting job, but it was worth a shot. And even more, my project wasn't actually due for another day. But my parents were going to be at the hospital with Emily, and that meant me, Frankie and Ashley would have the whole flat to ourselves.

Let that sink in.

THE WHOLE FLAT TO OURSELVES.

We'd been planning for weeks, saving up all our pocket money for the most extravagant pizza and ice-cream party in history. We were calling it "Uncle Hank's Grand Pizza and Ice-Cream Gala, and Soirée." Mum thought it was a study session, and, obviously, I would need to get to my boring history assignment, but it was the whole flat to ourselves!

My heart just wasn't in it for my sick-man act, but I didn't feel like giving up just yet. I hobbled over to the sofa and sat myself down very gingerly. Mum gave me the eye. "How do you expect to write your essay from the sofa?"

"I just need to ... gulp ... rest a little first."

"Hank, in this complex time, I need you to support your sister by finishing your history essay. Don't you agree, Stan?"

"I think you should put the book down for the night," Dad said to Mum, reaching for it. "You're starting to sound a little—"

She yanked it away. "And I think you should focus on being brave for your daughter."

"What's that supposed to mean?"

"You know how you are around anything medical."

"Calm and supportive?"

Mum flared her nostrils. "Stan, do you really want to get into it?" She reminded Dad that when it comes to blood, bruises, scabs and even twisted ankles, he's a huge baby. She also reminded him that while she was in labour with me, he was the one who needed to be sedated with goofy gas.

When they *really* started getting into it, I saw an opportunity to sneak off for a taste of ice cream. It felt cool and soothing on my inflamed tonsils.

"Hey! There she is!" my dad cried. "My brave little tiger cub! Raaaarrr!"

Emily had just materialized from the shadows. She very calmly walked over to the door and set down two neatly packed suitcases.

"How are you feeling, love?" Mum asked, shoving her hospital book under the cushions.

"It's only a tonsillectomy," Emily replied. "It's a very common and simple operation."

"I understand," Mum said.

"It's not a big deal. It's hardly an endoscopic bypass surgery or anything."

"No need to give all the medical details," Dad said.

"Well, love, I'm glad you're so calm," Mum said to Emily, raising an eyebrow at Dad.

"I'm calm," he said, and sidling over to Mum and putting an arm around her waist. "We both are."

"And supportive," Mum said. Then the two of them just looked at Emily with big, toothy fake smiles for what felt like for ever.

"I've packed some extra homework for myself," Emily said, "and some light reading material for Katherine in her bag."

"Oh love," Mum said, getting down on a knee and taking Emily's hand. "I know that your feelings must be very complex right now, and you know that your father and I would do anything to support you, but we can't take Katherine with us."

"Why not?"

"Because she's a lizard," Dad said.

From the kitchen, I snorted a laugh into my ice cream. Mum looked over and glared at me. "Hank, go to your room and support your sister. Now!"

CHAPTER FIVE

I went back to my room and sat at my desk.
I took out five fresh sheets of paper, glared
at all the white space for kind of a while,
then got my courage together and wrote
my name at the top.

Hank Zipzer.

It looked good, though a little plain. So
I made the "H" a block letter, and used
the rest of the page to sketch out more
variations of it.

Pretty soon it was almost 10 p.m. and my
eyelids were getting droopy. I found myself

drawing a new type of "Z" — I'd made it into kind of a lightning bolt zapping all the rest of the letters to dust. It was time to call it a night.

I hadn't exactly got the world's best jump on my essay. That was true. But I had everything ready, so I was all set to burst from the starting block — tomorrow. I had all day tomorrow. I mean, who starts a homework assignment more than twenty-four hours before it's due?

Crazy people, that's who.

I wasn't worried that tomorrow I had school all day, or that my evening was booked solid with "Uncle Hank's Grand Pizza and Ice-Cream Gala, and Soirée." I'd find an hour somewhere to knock out my essay. Five pages is nothing. Usually takes me no longer than forty-five minutes to knock out five pages.

I slept like a baby.

The first thing I did the next morning was open my desk drawer and count the wad of money I'd saved and collected from Ashley and Frankie. Between us we had almost *forty quid*, enough for an epic amount of pizza, ice cream, fizzy drinks, snacks and dessert. And if we needed a little more money, I knew the combination to Emily's lock box.

But wait, I know what you're thinking: isn't ice cream the dessert?

Of course we'd be having ice cream for dessert! But we'd also be serving it as an appetizer, and during the main course. It was all on the official menu:

UNCLE HANK'S GRAND PIZZA AND ICE-CREAM GALA, AND SOIRÉE

Formal attire requested

*****

18:00 to 18:30

Guests arrive; refreshments on ice

18:30 to 18:45

First course; mint-chocolate milkshakes

*****

18:45 to 19:00

Second course;

Hawaiian-style pizza from Fidel's

*****

19:00 to 19:15

Third course; more Hawaiian-style pizza

from Fidel's, side of ice cream

*****

19:15 to 19:45

Parlour games

*****

19:45 to 20:00

First dessert course;

guests may choose from either a triple-

scoop sundae or a triple-scoop banana split

*****

20:00 to 20:30

Music, dancing, festivities

20:30 to 20:45

Pizza-crust course; guests are encouraged to
dip their crusts into melted ice-cream soup

*****

20:45 to 21:00

Second dessert course;
ice cream with trick candles

*****

21:00 to ???

Third dessert course; sugar!!!!!!

I couldn't wait. There was no way I was
going to let a boring essay about depressing
World War I spoil the night to end all nights!

CHAPTER SIX

Teeth brushed, hair wild, uniform mostly
on, I gathered a pile of early versions of my
menu and my latest block letters, stuffed
them into a folder marked "World War I"
and burst into the living room, ready to
seize the day.

"Hank can do it," my dad said.

"You know it!" I said, still thinking about
day-seizing.

"No he can't," Emily said. "He can't even
look after himself."

"Of course I can do it," I said to Emily.

"You sure?" Dad asked.

"It's already done," I said and tapped my World War I folder, but nobody was paying much attention to me.

"He doesn't know the first thing about Lacertilia," Emily said.

"Sure I do," I blurted out, without waiting for any input from my brain. "Wait, what's this about a laser?"

"I don't know about this," Mum said, dragging her massive travel bags into the living room. "On top of looking after himself, now you want him to—"

"His friends will be with him," Dad said. "He'll be fine."

"Fine for what?"

"Do you feel calm and supported with this?" Mum asked Emily.

"Hardly," she said. "He doesn't know anything about her feeding habits."

"Huh?"

"Emily?" Dad asked. "Would you feel

33

more calm and supported if I didn't come to the hospital for your..."

"For her serious operation?" Mum said. "You're coming, Stan." Mum zipped up her bag.

"I guess it's settled then," he said.

"It is," she said.

"It is?" I said.

Emily sighed and skulked off into the hallway for her room.

With both bags around her shoulders, Mum came up to me. "So we'll be home before bedtime tomorrow. Tonight, Papa Pete will be here by 8."

"But you said 9."

"Fine." One of the straps on her bags slid down her shoulder and hung on her elbow. Just as she was about to knock over a lamp with her bag, I helped her with the strap. "Make sure you finish your essay tonight."

"Of course."

"And no junk food."

"I wouldn't dare," I said.

"And I left your dinner in the fridge."

"Here," said Emily, who had re-emerged silently from the hallway and put something plastic in my hand. It was a food storage tub. It took me a second, but then I noticed that something was moving behind the clear plastic, inside the container. Make that everything — every single thing inside the container was moving, creeping, writhing, clicking.

"Ahhh! What's wrong with you people?" I cried. "What's in this thing?"

"Dinner," Emily said. "Locusts and mealworms."

"Sounds delicious, Em, but I'm trying to cut back on mealworms."

"Ugh. If he's not going to take this seriously, then honestly..."

"Emily, I support your feelings," Mum said. "And so does your brother. But we have to get moving or we'll be late."

"But he—"

"Don't worry, love. Hank will do it."

"Fine," she sighed, and handed me a bulging folder.

"Do what?!" I said as they left, the door closing behind them. Then I looked more closely at the folder. It was labelled "Lizard Care and Feeding Schedule".

Wait! Had I just agreed to lizard-sit a walking handbag?

The door suddenly opened a crack, just enough for my sister to slide her collapsible head through the opening. "If anything happens to Katherine, I'll make your life a living nightmare."

I shook the plastic tub of locusts and mealworms. "Don't worry, sis. It already is."

CHAPTER SEVEN

I was so frazzled by everything that had just happened that without realizing it I left the flat still holding Katherine's dinner. It wasn't until I'd gone down the lift with Frankie and Ashley and we'd walked at least halfway to school that Frankie noticed the moving contents in my plastic tub.

He shrieked so loudly. "What's wrong with you?"

"What's wrong with me? These locusts are Emily's. She's the weird one."

"Sure, Hank, but why are you...?"

Exasperated, Ashley gestured at my container.

"'Cos I'm lizard-sitting Katherine. Obviously!"

"What I think we want to know is," Frankie said, "why are you holding that horrific thing?"

I shrugged. "You wanna hold it?"

"I don't think *anyone* should hold it."

"You probably should hold it," Ashley told Frankie. "Hank isn't always good at holding things."

"That's right," I said.

"And since it's only a matter of time before he drops it," Ashley went on, "those locusts in there will get out and wreak havoc on London."

"So basically, Frankie," I said, "either you hold it, or I unleash Emily's locusts and destroy the world."

Frankie stopped and put up his hands. "Let me repeat my question: why are you holding Emily's locusts?!"

"That's not important right now," I said.

"It isn't?"

"No. What's important is that Phase One of Operation Party Time is complete. Emily's gone to the hospital. And that means we've only got ten more hours until Phase Two: Go Nuts at Uncle Hank's Grand Pizza and Ice-Cream Gala!"

"And Soirée!" Ashley cried. "Can't wait."

"Too bad about taking care of Emily's spooky lizard," Frankie said.

"It is what it is," I said, shrugging. I looked at all those worms and clicking locusts writhing around in there. I didn't want to take care of the lizard, and those creatures probably didn't want to be Katherine's dinner. "I guess you can't always get what you want," I said. "We want the flat all to ourselves for our pizza and ice-cream social. But Emily wants creepy Katherine to be alive and nourished when she gets back from surgery. So you have to meet in the middle and fight it out. It's a lot like trench warfare, really."

"No, it isn't," Frankie said.

"You're right, Frankie," I said, without really hearing him because I was so inspired by my idea. "I think I'll write my essay on that, how Emily and I are..."

"You haven't started?" Ashley said.

"I finished it last night," I said, on autopilot. "Well, I *started* it last night. I mean, I *nearly* started last night. In fact, I've been nearly starting it for days. Check out this brilliant lightning-bolt 'Z' I came up with—" I zipped open my bag to get out my World War I folder. But as I did so, Emily's Lizard Care and Feeding Schedule folder came spilling out instead, and since my brain is only interested in moving things that are right in front of my eyes, I snatched for the falling folder, letting go of Emily's box of horrors...

And just before that revolting tub was about to crash into the unforgiving pavement, Frankie dived to the ground and scooped it up with both hands, saving our fair city from certain ruin. "Phew!"

"1-2-3-no-swapsies!" I called, and jumped up with a fist pump.

"That's so totally unfair," Frankie said, and I could tell he was searching for a way to get out of it. But I also knew Frankie: 1-2-3-no-swapsies was ironclad. He was an honourable mate, and to try to weasel out of no-swapsies was something not even a lizard would stoop to.

"But what am I gonna do with this at school?" he asked, trying to find a place in his bag to stash it.

"Tell Miss Adolf it's your lunch," I said.

Frankie shot me a lifted eyebrow.

"Seriously, that was my plan," I said. "Emily is always saying how we should be eating insects for our protein. It's more stainable for the environment."

"You mean 'sustainable'," Ashley said.

"Yeah. It's more sustainable than eating chickens and cows. Emily's always talking about starting an insect protein business. She thinks she could make millions by breeding all these insects, grinding them into powder, then selling the powder to people who make sausages and hamburgers. She says it's the future."

"Your sister has issues," Frankie said, eyeing the plastic tub with disgust.

"That's why they sent her to the hospital," I said. "Where she belongs."

We crossed the street. Westbrook Academy was in sight. I could hear all the kids yelling from the playground.

"I hope," Ashley said, "that they let Emily bring home her tonsils so I can examine them."

CHAPTER EIGHT

From the pages of Emily's Zipzer's field notebook...

9:31 a.m., 10th April

I've come to the hospital this morning
for a tonsillectomy. I feel perfectly calm.
My tonsils have been a nuisance since I
can remember, always getting inflamed,
elevating my body temperature, disrupting
my homework cycle. I have no idea why my
tonsils attract so many germs. I wonder if,

over the years, all of those extra germs have fused with me. Perhaps they've even given me greater cognitive powers. I wonder what not having them in my body will be like.

I've requested to keep my extracted tonsils for further study. Nurse Adebayor and others are reviewing my request.

I wanted to keep this field notebook primarily to document my experiences, and to jot down any impressions I may have about the procedure and the larger health care system in general.

But since last night, I haven't had a calm moment to reflect on anything. The reason is simple: Mum and Dad. Their actions over the past twenty-four hours make me question whether parents should be allowed to take responsibility for a child without first passing a battery of psychological tests.

My parents give me no rest. The mother is obsessed with some ridiculous paperback book she found at the bus terminal called *Taking Your Child to the Hospital*, and the father is totally consumed by a neurotic fear of anything medical.

Both, however, project all their fears and anxieties onto me. They think they are trying to help me, but instead are making me — I who am about to go under the knife — responsible for their emotional well-being. They try to tell me to "think happy thoughts", they try to have "little chats" with me in "clear and reassuring language", and, rather than calming them, my stoic demeanour makes them even more insecure and hysterical about their parenting.

Ugh!

If only Katherine were here. She asks nothing of me, needs nothing more than locusts and a heat lamp, says nothing, feels nothing — a perfect companion!

I was not allowed to bring her. For what reason, I have no idea. She is a perfectly clean reptile. Much cleaner than the father.

It's unfair. They let other animals come and provide support. Ah, but those must be service animals. I will have to apply to get Katherine made a service animal. They let all sorts of filthy mammals become service animals these days. Why not a very clean and conscientious reptile?

Oh, poor Katherine. She should be here with me, instead of at home with the brother – Hank. I fear for the worst.

10:57 a.m.

Mum tried to explain how the "nice doctors" were going to give me "goofy gas" so I could "drift off into a lovely deep sleep". I have no idea what she is talking about.

Meanwhile, I have more important things to think about, as the medical staff will soon be coming in to administer my anaesthetic. I am intrigued. I wonder how it will feel to be under the anaesthetic. Will I have any awareness? Any concept of self? Of passing time?

The parents seem very stressed about the situation. Surely knowledge would provide the greatest comfort, so I tried to reassure them: I informed them that the anaesthetic will most likely be delivered through an intravenous cannula on the back of my hand.

The father's legs buckled and he nearly collapsed into the biohazard bin.

CHAPTER NINE

The final bells rang, the doors flew open and a lot of kids around London became much happier. I certainly was. Tonight was going to be the best night of my life.

But I still had lots to do to get ready.

Frankie, Ashley and I raced back home to our building. Frankie had taken good care of Emily's plastic tub all day, keeping it hidden in his dark and warm bag — perfect breeding conditions. He gave it back to me as we got out of the lift. They were going to finish up their projects before party time at six, and

I had to do that as well, plus get the party preparations done. A pizza and ice-cream soirée doesn't just happen on its own, you know.

I had the entire flat all to myself. And since that's such a rare thing, I thought I'd revel in it a bit. As soon as I got home, I dropped all my stuff and laid down smack in the middle of the living room, spreading my arms and legs as wide as they'd go.

But no matter how hard I tried, I couldn't relax. I had too much to do. I kept hearing my brain making lists, and since that really stressed me out, every time I heard my brain making a list, I yawned and stretched out and flushed the list from my brain, trying to get myself nice and relaxed before starting on my duties.

I knew I had to do between one and nine things. I had to feed Katherine, do my essay and prepare the social. But since those last two things were actually countless different things, I decided I'd get the one thing out of the way first. The thought of doing that thing really stressed me out, and it took me at least an hour of just lying there until I was ready.

I grabbed the locust tub and Emily's folder, and creaked open the door to Emily's room, half expecting to trigger a mustard-gas booby trap.

No gas. Only the weird and sour smell of Emily's room.

The first thing I saw in Emily's room was Katherine's eyes. The creepy lizard was staring right at me. She — or was it an it? — was sitting motionless on Emily's pillow, like she was waiting for me. I froze. The lizard flicked out its tongue and licked its own eyeball.

"I bet you must be hungry for ... locusts. Ew!"

I looked down at the writhing tub. Then I looked back at the motionless lizard. How was I supposed to do this? Was I supposed to hand feed that thing one of those writing bugs? But how would I get one of them out without letting them all out? Was I supposed to actually touch one of those things? Could I use something — like Emily's tweezers — to get the locusts out?

The lizard licked its other eyeball.

I consulted Emily's bulging folder of instructions. Emily's details were detailed ... very detailed. They started with some in-depth background on the lizard. Her report began over 300 million years ago, when the very first lizard emerged from a goopy pond and slithered onto land...

"Sorry, Katherine," I yawned. "You're just not that interesting."

The lizard looked at me.

"You're gonna have to help yourself tonight," I said, and set down the tub on the floor by the bed. "If you can open the box, they're all yours."

I checked my phone. It was 4:30 p.m. Plenty of time before six to get the ice cream, fizzy drinks and snacks, order the pizzas and start my essay. I splashed some ice-cold water on my face, let out one of my getting-down-to-business shrieks, and while Ms DeLillo was furiously knocking on her ceiling in the flat below with her broomstick, I ordered the pizzas, telling the guy at Fidel's to deliver them at exactly 5:55 p.m. sharp.

Then I grabbed our precious savings and jogged down to the corner shop, where I bought so many buckets of ice cream, bottles of fizzy drinks and snacks that they had to get a cardboard box from the storeroom so I could carry it all.

Back to the flat at 5:10, I stowed all the perishables and meltables, set out Mum's second-best plates, spread out some board games, and, with forty minutes to go, went to my room to get a jump start on my essay.

I didn't jump very far. I was so angry at Miss Adolf for making this ridiculous essay due the day after the best night ever that, although I had every intention of writing a few well-structured paragraphs about trench warfare, I wound up just making a silly drawing of her. She had the body of a Venus flytrap, plenty of beauty spots on her semi-human face, and lightning was threatening to strike from the storm clouds above.

I had just put my last beauty spot on her nose when I looked up. It was 5:50. I clapped my hands and got up to change into my party finest. I put on the black blazer I'd worn to my great-great uncle's funeral last winter. I found some string and tied it around my antique Casio calculator watch and stuck it in my pocket. There, pocket watch sorted! Then I went into the living room, tuned the radio to some station playing very sophisticated bossa nova tunes and poured myself a cola with ice. For the last few minutes, I lounged around with my drink, revelled in the classy, relaxed vibe and waited for the pizza man.

CHAPTER TEN

Frankie arrived first, at exactly 6:01. I swung out my watch from my pocket, glanced at it and turned my attention to my mate.

He had on a black top hat and white gloves.

"Welcome, good sir," I said. "May I trouble you for the password?"

Frankie pulled out something on a chain from *his* blazer and put it up to his eye. It was a monocle! "Cheerio," he said.

"Very good, sir. Won't you come in?"

"Charming, charming," Frankie said, like

he couldn't be more bored, looking around through his monocle as he strode in. "I like what you've done with the place."

"Allow me to take your hat, mate."

"Certainly."

While Frankie breathed on his monocle and cleaned it on his sleeve, I flung his top hat into the corner, spinning it with a flick of my wrist.

"Ah, and there's Ashley," I said. An incredibly tall girl was standing in my doorway. Ashley was wearing heels! She was taller than my dad in her evening dress and heels, and with the feather sticking out from her complicated hat, she almost had to hunch to get in the doorway.

"Cheerio," she said.

"Simply delightful," I said as I helped her out of her gloves.

She opened up her little clutch handbag and pulled out a large metal bottle. "A little something for tonight's festivities," she said and gave it to me. "It's the finest whipped cream in all of Her Majesty's kingdom."

"Splendid!" I said. "Won't you both sit down for a refreshment."

"We'd be delighted," Frankie said.

While they found seats on the sofa, I poured them colas. "I'm so glad you could make it to my little impromptu gathering. I must apologize that the place is in such a state. The servants have just been dreadful of late." I came round the sofa and handed out the drinks. "Cheers then."

We clinked, and sipped.

"So tell me, Frankie," I started, "how've you been getting on with your studies?"

"Splendidly, Hank."

"And you, Ashley?" I said. "I hear tell that yours are going quite well, too."

"Oh, I've nothing to complain about," Ashley said. She kicked off her heels, twirled them around on her fingers and let them fly into the corner with Frankie's top hat. "Should we crack open that bottle of whipped cream, then?"

I swung out my timepiece. "I don't see why not."

CHAPTER ELEVEN

Just as I was stuffing the 49th piece of popcorn into my mouth without swallowing any of them, I heard a beeping sound. I'd actually been aware of it since the 23rd piece of popcorn, but every time I asked my mates if they heard it too, no one could understand me.

"Does anyone else hear that?" Frankie finally asked.

"I WOO!" I cried, and all 49 pieces of popcorn came flying from my mouth in a tidal wave onto a metre-high pile of rubbish that covered the floor. "It's Dad's laptop!" I said. "No one panic. No one panic!"

I dug through pizza boxes, wet popcorn, cola bottles, whipped cream and a million other small and broken things on the floor for the laptop.

Uncle Hank's Grand Pizza and Ice-Cream Gala had been a smashing success, not to mention the soirée. We had feasted till we could feast no more. We had poured three flavours of ice cream down our throats. We had danced, made merry, and I had won three out of four eating and wrestling contests. I had even, on a dare from Frankie, drunk a smoothie he'd made using everything we'd had to eat tonight, with a healthy serving of Ashley's whipped cream of course, and also three dabs of a mysterious greenish paste that Frankie had found in the back of the cupboard. The smoothie was delicious! It was a night to end all nights.

And oh the whipped cream, did it flow!

And now, the night to end all nights was coming to a sudden and panic-inducing end. Plus the mysterious greenish paste wasn't sitting too well in my gut. Frankie couldn't be sure that it was edible *exactly*, but you know how I am with eating things that aren't really food.

I found Dad's laptop under a mountain of pizza boxes. I flicked off a hunk of pineapple from the screen. "It's my mum! On video call! I'm panicking. Guys, I'm panicking!"

The entire living room was covered with a solid metre of party fouls. I picked up the laptop, my eyes scanning desperately for somewhere cleanish to take it and answer the call. I looked to the kitchen. That too had seen better days. Frankie hadn't exactly tidied up while making his smoothie.

That left my room. Unfortunately it was filled with popcorn, from our no-holds-barred popcorn royal rumble.

Mum's room. That too was destroyed, after I'd torn through Dad's wardrobe trying to find a cravat to one-up Frankie's monocle.

The bathroom. That was too weird a place to answer the call, plus I didn't want anyone to see my shaving-cream-and-greenish-paste sculpture — not until it had dried, anyway.

The hallway. Too suspicious. Why would I just be hanging out in the hallway?

Emily's room. Ditto.

I'd have to work some Zipzer magic. "Clear a path! Make like a street-sweeper and clear a path!" I called out to my regiment of well-dressed guests. While they spread their wings and pushed the piles of rubbish to the walls, I found the tallest chair in the flat, set the laptop on it, and put a bunch of my rubber-soldiers under the laptop to angle the screen up so that the person on the other end couldn't possibly see the floor.

Everything set, I flipped the radio to some classical piano, drank the last of the everything-smoothie and accepted the call. "Hi there, Mum!"

CHAPTER TWELVE

"Where's Katherine?"

Two beady little eyes, magnified behind glasses, stared at me from the laptop screen. Emily. "Oh, it's you."

"How is she? Has her anxiety rash flared up? Put her on. I want to speak to her."

"You've..." I did everything in my power to keep my eyes from looking *shifty* and glanced around for a clue. I had put Ashley on lizard duty at the beginning of the night, and she was presently flipping through page after page of Emily's lizard care notes.

"You've just missed her," I said.

Emily wasn't buying it. "You haven't checked on her once, have you?"

"'Course I have," I said, and wheeled my hand at Ashley to hurry up. Finally she held up a sheet of paper to me, covered in microscopic words that were dancing and playing leap-frog. I squinted and tried to freeze everything in place, but everything was a gelatinous swirl. "I uhh, err..."

Thankfully Ashley saw my squinty look. She grabbed a marker, flipped the pages over and wrote something on the back in huge block letters. "I... I put her to bled."

"She's bleeding? Is her mouth rot coming back? What have you—"

"Bed, bed. I put her to bed."

"I don't believe you. What were you looking at? Why am I looking up at you from below your chin? Mum, Hank is an unfit guardian. We have to go home."

Everything shook as my family appeared

to fight over the phone. Finally my dad's face filled the screen. He was wearing a surgical mask, which he pulled down below his neck. "No, we don't. You're taking good care of her, aren't you, Hank?"

"Of course," I said. "Why are you wearing a surgical mask?"

But my dad didn't have time to answer. Everything shook again till my mum had wrested back control of her phone.

"Hank, have you eaten?"

"Ask him why we're looking up at him?" I heard Emily say off screen.

"I hope you've finished your project," Mum said, and looked around with mum eyes, scanning my face and the whole view for anything suspect. "Why am I looking up your nose?"

"I'm downloading something for school," I said without missing a beat. Mum is an expert at spotting lies, but she's useless with computers. "I have to keep the laptop at this angle or I'll sever the uplink."

"That's not true," I heard Emily say.

"I really should jump off now," I said, clicking a bunch of keys on the keyboard. "This call is eating into my bandwidth, and my JavaScript is unstable enough as it is."

I saw my mum thinking. She seemed to buy it, for now. "Have the others gone home yet?"

Both of them leaned in behind me and waved for the camera, all smiles. "Hi, Mrs Zipzer!"

"How did it go?" Ashley asked. "Did they use a high-energy laser, or was it a cold-steel procedure?"

In the background, behind Mum, I saw Dad call for the nurse and draw the mask up over his mouth again.

"Neither," Mum said. "They've delayed the operation till tomorrow."

"Oh, could you ask the doctor if Emily can keep the tonsils?" Ashley asked.

"I've already put in a request," Emily said from behind Mum.

Just then, Frankie tripped a bit on the side of a pizza box, tried to catch himself, but wound up throwing out his arms and flailing to the ground in a crash of debris.

"What's that?"

"Doorbell, Mum, Papa Pete's here."

"No it wasn't," Emily said.

"Emily sounds tired, and scared. Better support her. I gotta get the door. Bye Mum, talk tomorrow. Nice chat. Bye."

"Is Frankie wearing my cravat...?" my dad was saying, but with a flick of my finger I cut off the call, dived to the floor and breathed an extra-large sigh of relief.

CHAPTER THIRTEEN

"Think they bought it?" Frankie asked, as we got up and brushed pizza sauce and popcorn kernels from our formal attire.

I shrugged. "Does it matter? They're not going to leave Emily in her time of need. And once we're done tidying up this place, it'll be like it never happened."

"We?" Ashley said.

"Oh come on."

"Yup," Frankie yawned and stretched. "Better get home and hit the hay."

Ashley followed suit, yawning and rubbing

her eyes.

"You guys can't be serious," I said. "Who's going to help me with my history project?"

"You know it's due tomorrow morning, right?" Ashley told me.

I nodded meekly.

"Hate to say it, dude," Frankie said, "but this time you're in deep."

And then I felt my life force drip out of my ear. I'd done it again!

I crumbled to the floor and curled around a pizza box. "How am I gonna do three weeks of work in one night? With my brain?" I yawned. "And now my brain is really sleepy, too!"

Ashley and Frankie did their best to reassure me, reminding me that I usually come up with something in trying times like these. But just as I was thinking that yes, maybe I had a shot, they told me about their projects. Ashley had made a medical study of the effects of gangrene, trench foot and other war wounds, while Frankie had made some annotated graphic depictions of major battles for his presentation.

"I'm so dead," I said. I picked up a crust of pizza and hurled it at the picture of Miss Adolf I'd drawn earlier and tacked to the wall. It hit her square in her nose, ricocheted off the wall and flew directly into my left eye. "Ow!"

"Hank!" a voice barked. I looked through my fingers to see Papa Pete standing in the doorway with his hands on his hips, shaking his head. "What's a matter with you, eh?"

In silence, he marched through the living room straight to the table, past the carnage, and prodded a piece of pineapple in the pizza box, frowning. "Is that pineapple?"

"Uh—"

"You put pineapple on a pizza?!" He sniffed at the pineapple, reared back in disgust, then took a bite of a slice. He shook his head slowly as he chewed with

71

great disapproval, before going over to the sink and letting the regurgitated bite drop from his mouth. He rinsed his mouth out thoroughly. "Who put pineapple on the pizza?"

"We got it from Fidel's."

"Fidel, eh?" He picked up the kitchen phone and dialled. I called out to him, but he put up his finger. "Fidel?" he asked. "It's Pete. What's a matter with you? Eh? You know what you did. You put pineapple on a pizza! A pineapple has no place on a pizza. It's disgraceful, Fidel. Disgraceful. My grandson is sick from it. He's on the floor right now..."

"But Papa Pete..." He put up his finger again and winked at me.

"You'll bake another and send it right over? Good. And put it in the stone oven. Twelve minutes and basta! And Fidel, if I catch you putting pineapple on a pizza again, I'll come over there myself. OK? Say hello to your mama for me. OK, *buona notte*."

He hung up with a smile.

"Awesome!" Ashley yelled.

"Pizza! Pizza!" Frankie chanted.

"So, why wasn't I invited?" Papa Pete asked, waving his hand around the flat.

"Sorry, Papa Pete," I said. "It was kids only. But now it's over. Frankie and Ashley are really tired."

"No we're not!" they both protested.

"But I am." I went over to the corner and retrieved Frankie's hat and Ashley's heels, and handed them back as I walked my friends to the door. "And I have to get down to business."

"Here," Frankie said, handing me the monocle. "Use it wisely."

CHAPTER FOURTEEN

After Frankie and Ashley had left, and after
Fidel himself had personally brought over
a piping hot pizza, Papa Pete and I sat and
talked over my third dinner of the night.
I told him everything. I can talk to Papa
Pete about this stuff, and I never feel like
I have to lie or bend the truth. My parents
used to get really angry at me, before we
learned about all my weird brain issues. And
though they've been more understanding
lately, I can still feel pretty defective when

these things come up. Like they secretly want a better version of me or something. Sometimes it can even feel like I'm some sort of giant bug that can't do anything right. I mean, they're always trying to get me to go on all these special diets and buying me all these educational video games and — well, it can get tiring, and I feel so bad when I let them down because I know they're trying...

But Papa Pete is someone I can talk to about it. Sure, he's not thrilled when I tell him that I procrastinated for three weeks. But he knows that I'm trying. OK, so I don't always really try. But even when I don't try, I don't feel like I'm a bad person in front of Papa Pete. So I told him all about the latest hole I'd dug for myself.

"This is terrible, Hank."

"I'm really sorry, Papa Pete."

"The pizza, Hank, the pizza. Fidel is ... I'm going to have to call his mama."

"But what am I gonna do? Don't you know a lot about World War I?"

"Why would you think that?"

"Weren't you in the war? Maybe I can interview you about it."

"World War I?"

"Yeah," I said.

"How old do you think I am, Hank?"

I shrugged.

"Hank, when was World War I?"

I shrugged again.

"I think we have our work cut out for us. Come on, Hank. Let's get this place tidied up, then we'll see about your project. You'll think of something, but first get up and get the blood flowing, eh?"

I slumped to the table. "Papa, I don't have time to tidy ... and do my project! And look after locust breath!"

"Who?"

"Wait — where is she? Where is Katherine?"

I had the Zipzer sense that something was deeply and madly wrong. Ashley had gone into Emily's room earlier to check up on the walking shoe-leather, but from my seat at the table, I saw that Emily's door was still open a crack. I was doomed!

"Oh no," I screamed as I ran over and threw open the door, hoping to see those creepy eyes staring back at me from the pillow. I even half expected to see a skin-suit that Katherine had moulted out of. But all I saw was the pillow. And on the floor, the writhing tub of locusts.

I checked everywhere in Emily's room. Under the bed. Under the covers. In her closet, where she keeps a stereo that is always on, playing jungle sounds. I checked all the drawers. In her wardrobe. I picked up the locust container and shook it, scanning around and calling out, "Dinner!"

Oh man. I only had ten hours before the first lesson tomorrow, and the last thing I needed at that moment was to be crawling around on the floor trying to sniff out a dinosaur. I tried to imagine that I had a lizard-mind-meld superpower, and, thinking just like a lizard, I squirmed around and checked all the places a lizard would hide.

But I didn't have lizard-man superpowers. And I was running out of time. I ran into the living room. "No, no, no," I shouted to Papa Pete. "I can't lose Katherine. Emily'll eat me alive if I lose her."

"Uh, Hank?"

"Come on, Papa Pete. Don't just stand there," I said and got on my hands and knees, peering under the sofa. "Help me!"

"Hank?"

"What?"

Papa Pete was pointing at the sofa. I followed his finger, looked up, saw nothing, and shrugged.

"Look closer."

Something strange clicked in my brain

somewhere. I blinked. Then I saw an eye, a creepy yellow rock of an eye, looking right into mine. The eye was ten inches from mine. The eye was Katherine's. She was sitting on the sofa without a care in the world.

"Have you been there this whole time? I couldn't see you!"

Then something strange clicked in another part of my brain.

"Hold on ... I couldn't see you 'cos ... I've got it! I know what to do for my project. Thank you, sweet Katherine."

Then I had kind of an out-of-body experience, seeing myself from overhead. I watched myself lean in and give Katherine a big wet kiss on the lips, or whatever those things are. Then I snapped back into myself, just in time to watch Katherine lick her eyeball.

"Gross! I'm becoming Emily!"

CHAPTER FIFTEEN

From the pages of Emily Zipzer's field notebook...

10:21 p.m.

I have just been informed by Nurse Adebayor that my procedure has been pushed back until tomorrow morning. My surgeon, Dr Anita Henkes, has been tied up treating a youth who managed to stick a coloured pencil all the way up his nose. I cannot quite fathom the youth's stupidity.

Nor can I fathom how the NHS could be so inefficient. Here I am presently in a bed, a bed which I've taken up all day, a bed which another sick patient must need and cannot get. My sitting here is likely costing the system a great deal of money. Wasted money. I plan to request the NHS's records when I get back, and make a full audit of their data and patient processing systems.

While I've been thinking about efficiency and databases, the parents have been arguing about who gets to spend the night on the sole fold-out camp bed. The father wants to prove to the mother that he isn't afraid of hospitals, and the mother, I presume, must have something to prove to that ridiculous book. Neither wants to be here, neither needs to be here, yet both are fighting for the privilege of sleeping on the dinky roll-away bed. Absurd.

Even more absurd: we just got off a video call with Hank. The brother has clearly not checked on Katherine even once. In our short conversation, Hank made three obvious lies. And yet neither one of my parents feels the need to head back to the flat, and instead are fighting tooth and nail to stay here, for no apparent reason.

I repeat: FOR NO APPARENT REASON.

"Is it possible not to let either parent stay?" I asked Nurse Adebayor. But before the nurse could answer my question and best see to *my* needs, both parents insisted that they would be staying. Even though there's only a bed for one of them.

Oh joy.

1:34 a.m.

Have yet to catch a wink of sleep, thanks to the parents. Mum is sleeping in the camp bed. Every time she moves, the bed moves on its creaky wheels.

The father, meanwhile, is making an

absurd attempt to sleep in a chair. Every time his head leans back too far, he snorts, wakes himself up, mumbles "who's there?" and then very gradually tilts his head back further and further until he snorts himself awake once again.

I doubt I will get any sleep tonight. There is a reason that, as a present for my second birthday, I asked to stop being forced to sleep in their bed, instead preferring to share mine with the calm and supportive presence of a reptile.

CHAPTER SIXTEEN

My idea was perfect. It was better than perfect. It was so good that Miss Adolf would probably go into shock upon seeing the results tomorrow. She'd go into shock, have to be taken to the hospital to be treated alongside Emily, and then my favourite teacher, Mr Rock, would substitute for her. All. Week. Long.

Want to know my better-than-perfect idea?

Camouflage. You know, the ability to disappear into your surroundings.

Camouflage, the superpower I've really
wanted my whole life.

And it was all thanks to Katherine.

I didn't know much about military
camouflage, but I knew enough to know
that it had to be new-*ish*. I knew that way
back in the day they used to fight battles
like crazy people. The two sides would
wear bright uniforms, get into two lines
facing each other and then just start firing
weapons.

But World War I was different. During that
war, they tried to get out of the way. They
dug those trenches. And during that war,
they must have come up with camouflage.

After looking it up online, it turned out
that they didn't *exactly* invent camouflage
during World War I. The idea had been
around for a little while, but they *had* come
up with the *name* for camouflage during
World War I. The word was French, and it
meant blowing smoke in someone's eyes.

But they didn't actually use camouflage that much during the war.

"It didn't work so well," Papa Pete said. "But the French wasted a lot of time camouflaging outposts and painting their faces. If they had stopped all that silliness, we could have taken the Alps in the summer of '17."

"What do you mean, 'we'?" I asked Papa Pete. "I thought you said you weren't in the—"

"I wasn't, Hank," he said as he walked over to the window and looked out at the moon. "I wasn't..."

Normally I would have tried to get to the bottom of Papa Pete's mysterious past, but my mind was stuck on my camouflage project. It wasn't perfect. But I could camouflage the fact that it wasn't perfect with a cool presentation. And with my cool presentation, I could camouflage the fact that for three weeks I hadn't done diddly-squat on my camouflage project.

Yes, it was perfect!

But it was also a lot of hard work. Papa Pete helped me all the way through. We worked together on it, going through old encyclopaedias and Internet sites, taking notes, organizing them, and then he helped me put all my thoughts into words.

I learned a ton about the war. It was fascinating and grisly. I never could understand why it started in the first place, but I learned that at the time, everyone thought they needed to fight, and that the war would be over quickly. But that's not how it happened. It just became this gruesome stalemate, with both sides dug into their trenches. In a major battle, one side might only gain just a few hundred feet.

"Why did they keep fighting, Papa Pete?"

"Because Hank," he said, getting up from the computer. He walked over to the window and gazed off into the moonlight again. "Because, Hank, man is an insane animal..."

"You sure you weren't in the war, Papa Pete?"

He didn't answer, just kept staring off at the moon and clouds. Maybe Papa Pete really was in the war! Or maybe it was just really late. We worked on the essay until two o'clock in the morning, and when that was done, I finally got started on my presentation.

Katherine sat on my pillow and watched us working in the lamplight the whole time. At one point, in a daze and my eyes blurry, I even screwed up the courage to hand feed her a locust. I cracked open the plastic container, grabbed a stickly leg and pulled a fluttering locust out. Katherine gobbled it right out of my hand, and I could tell she was thankful. It was almost sweet.

CHAPTER SEVENTEEN

I slept no more than two hours. Katherine slept on my nightstand, on a nest she had made out of my undies. At least I think she was sleeping. It's hard to tell with lizards. I'm not even sure if whatever they do at night is called sleeping. It might be called something else. I'd have to ask Emily about it.

Strike that. I'll just look it up online, and then erase the search from my browser forever. Better to avoid giving Emily a chance to deliver a long-winded lecture on the living habits of lizards. It would only encourage her.

When Frankie and Ashley came by to pick me up for school, I was still asleep with Katherine, and Papa Pete told them he'd be taking me to school. Papa Pete was still grouchy about Fidel's pizza, and all while he was making coffee and breakfast for us, and helping me double check everything with red eyes, I could hear him muttering beneath his breath about the outrage of baking tropical fruit in cheese.

I felt like I was in Miss Adolf's gas mask, with everything seeming blurry and far away. Papa Pete guided me around the flat, helped me to get my bag together and carried my project down to his car. As soon as the back of my head touched the headrest of my seat, I was out like a light.

When he had dropped me off, I began to wake up. And seeing the project in my arms, I was feeling really good about everything. I knew the material inside out. I could hear it looping around in my brain. Camouflage was all I could think about, the only thing I'd seen all morning. I saw worms blending into the dirt, pigeons blending into buildings, kids in school uniforms blending into kids in school uniforms. And I realized something: everyone and everything was scared of being noticed, of sticking out. Because sticking out meant getting eaten. At least for animals. I really started to feel for all the animals out there, even the locusts in that disgusting tub. I mean, if you're a locust, everything wants to eat you, just for being alive. Talk about a mad situation.

I was so busy thinking about all this crazy stuff that I didn't realize that I had walked right past Miss Berkson, the school administrator, and she hadn't noticed me at all, so no late slip! Maybe I was starting to blend in?

Miss Adolf didn't notice me either when I slipped into my classroom and over to my seat. She was squeaking something out on the board.

But my mates noticed me, and my project. It would be hard not to. It was made of three pizza boxes and took up my entire desk. Maybe my camouflage powers only worked on adults?

"Wait," Ashley said. "You actually did your project?"

"In one night?" Frankie said.

"No problem," I said. "Papa Pete helped with the words. And it's got a great presentation." I patted the pizza boxes and got that gruesome plastic tub out of my bag.

"I see you brought the locusts again," Frankie said, inching slowly away from me. "There's no way on earth I'm holding it again—"

"Relax, Frankie," I said. "I meant to bring it this time."

"Why?"

"Hank?" Ashley asked. "Is there a lizard in those pizza boxes?"

"Hank?"

"She's camouflaged. It's brilliant, right? That's what my project's on — the use of camouflage in trench warfare. It was Katherine's idea." I opened up the plastic container a fraction of an inch, pinched out a tiny mealworm, and slipped it through a crack in my pizza box presentation. A tongue grabbed it and sucked it in.

"Did he just say it was Katherine's idea?" Frankie asked Ashley.

"And did he really just feed a lizard a worm?" Ashley asked Frankie.

"Like I say — brilliant."

Ashley reminded me of a certain fact, however. "Except in Emily's instructions, it was written that under no circumstances should you take Katherine out of the flat."

"Emily says a lot of things I don't listen to. Why start now? But I do think she's onto something with her insect protein business. Could be the future. Right, Katherine?"

I fed the lizard another mealworm.

CHAPTER EIGHTEEN

**From the pages of Emily Zipzer's field
notebook...**

9:45 a.m.

The father has awoken to severe back pain.
No surprise there, considering he slept in an
NHS chair. He smiles through the pain, but
every time he so much as turns his head, I
hear a sound like snapping twigs.

The doctor, Anita, just came in to
introduce herself. She is an Ear, Nose and

Throat clinician, and, one hopes, also a surgeon. I did notice, however, that the nail polish on her left hand was somewhat uneven. Perhaps she simply went to a bad manicurist. Or perhaps her hands shake, which, alarmingly, could be an early sign of palsy.

But it is such a simple procedure. A dentist could do it. It will only take 25 to 35 minutes, though the recovery generally lasts two to three hours. Anita was so impressed with my medical knowledge that she made a condescending remark about my becoming a doctor when I'm all grown up.

As if! I might as well be a landscaper.

While I was imagining my future as a nuclear physicist or a quantum mathematician, the mother read excerpts from her ridiculous book to Anita about how I was a very confused and emotionally fragile young girl. And then, when Mum and Dad were arguing about Mum's pathetic obsession with her book, the doctor mentioned the world "needle", and the father emitted a high-pitched shriek and tried to make a run for it.

He hadn't run three feet before he crashed into the biohazard bin, and splashed half the room with yellow juice.

12:39 p.m.

They have just administered the anaesthetic. It was painless. The father turned green and hid his eyes in Mum's skirts while the needle went in. And then the mother fainted to the floor.

That is all I have time to mention right now. They want to take my notebook away from me. I feel sleepy. I will fight it. I will make a part of myself stay lucid and aware even under the anaesthetic. This is too interesting an experience to miss completely. I must stay awake. I mussssssssssssssss...

2:13 p.m.

I heard them working on me the whole time.
Believe it or not, but I heard them. I felt
no pain. I tried to communicate with the
outside world by moving my eyelids in Morse
code, but few medical staff, apparently,
are versed in it. They were listening to
Rachmaninoff's Piano Concerto No.2. Check
local radio playlists for proof that I was
aware during the procedure.

When I woke I could not speak. I could
only look around. So I observed.

While I was out, both parents had
received extensive medical care. The mother
had several bandages wrapped around her
head and was leaning back with an ice pack.
The father kept prodding the mother not
to nod off, as she most likely suffered a
concussion from the fall. The father, by the
way, was in a back brace, with one of his
arms held winged and aloft.

I was promised ice cream. Let it be known here that when I woke up, all of my post-surgery ice cream had been eaten.

Both deny it. Both are lying. I will get my revenge.

CHAPTER NINETEEN

Finally it was my turn to present to the class. Half asleep, I'd listened to kids get up and present project after boring project. None were even half as interesting as mine. Except for Ashley's. Her presentation on trench foot was really fascinating. Did you know that all it takes to get trench foot is to expose your feet to damp and cold air for too long? And then your feet start to rot, and before you know it, they have to amputate your feet. That's the only way to treat it. But if I got trench feet, I'd be, like, no, not me, you can't amputate my feet. My feet are fine. Just a bit stinky. Go amputate someone else's feet...

When I realized I was becoming so fascinated with trench foot that I was forgetting my own project, I zoned out again until it was my turn.

"Henry Zipzer," Miss Adolf said, gesturing to the front of the classroom. I felt all eyes on me and heard them whispering as I marched up there, carrying my project. Mine was by far the biggest. Miss Adolf tapped her lip and watched me with arched eyebrows the whole time.

"This is really a new low, Henry," Miss Adolf said as I plopped my pizza-box contraption down on her desk. "You can't really pretend that this is—"

"My presentation, Miss. You're going to love it."

"But Henry, you know I despise rubbish." Her face strained into that smile again where she's trying to smile, but her face muscles won't cooperate. McKelty burst out laughing.

But I paid them no attention. I got out my essay from my back pocket, unfolded it, cleared my throat several times, and gazed at all the letters that would just not stay put. My voice came soft and weak. "Soldiers in World War I got the idea of cam ... cam ... camouflage from animals that blend into the virus—I mean, the environment..."

I paused. I was starting to develop a stutter, but more than that, I knew those hazy words on the page were no match for how cool camouflage really was.

I set the notes down.

"Listen, there's some more stuff I wrote down here..."

"Which I will be grading," Miss Adolf said.

"But who needs words? What I have to show you is one of the coolest things nature has ever come up with. Ever wish you had a superpower? Like the power to be invisible? We all have. But animals do it all the time. They blend in and disappear before our very eyes. Don't believe me? Well, I've got a live demonstration. See it for yourself. Are you ready?"

"Yeah!" everyone said.

I started to open the box, then stopped and vamped it up a bit. "You guys aren't ready. Are you sure you're ready?"

"We're ready!" they cried.

"Open the box, Hank!" one kid named Maurice said. "Let's see what's in there!"

"You will." I twirled my hands about a bit. "Or will you?"

Very slowly, and with a magician's skill, I cracked open the box, inch by inch, revealing a diorama of a jungle scene, complete with sand and leaves and some foliage I took from Katherine's terrarium habitat. I opened the box and made a flourish with my hands. "Ta da!"

Silence.

"Congratulations, Henry, it's an empty box."

"Exactly, camouflage. Look again, but this time concentrate. Tell me what you see."

Miss Adolf stood from her chair. "I see a very disruptive young man who's about to get detention."

"You must be in shock, Miss," I said. "Clear your mind and see the box with new eyes."

"Hank!" Frankie stage whispered. "It really is an empty box!"

"Nonsense, Frankie," I replied, and came around the desk and looked in. Nope, I didn't see a thing. "Sometimes," I said, suddenly unsure but still projecting confidence, "these lizards are so camouflaged, that they are practically invisible. You must feel for them with your hands." I felt around, to a rising chorus of laughter. I felt nothing, other than my life force leaking out of my ear again.

"Oh, boy."

"You aren't fooling me, Henry."

"We've got to find her!" I cried, whipping my head around. There was a swirl of laughing faces and fingers pointing at me, but no lizard in sight.

"Henry, you simply cannot camouflage the fact that you failed to complete your assignment with this ruse."

"But it's Emily's lizard. We've got to find her! Everyone look by your feet!"

"Not even you would be irresponsible enough to bring a live lizard into this school."

"But Miss! I so would!"

"I'm giving you one week's detention for this ludicrous spectacle. Do you want another, for ludicrously lying about live lizards?"

"To be fair, Miss, the lizard may be dead."

Miss Adolf glared at me, grinding her teeth to chalk.

"There he is," McKelty shouted, and pointed at me. "Right before your eyes, the stupidest kid in all of Westbrook Academy."

There was nowhere to hide.

CHAPTER TWENTY

All morning long, I kept my eyes peeled for
Katherine. But I didn't spot her anywhere.
Not once. Emily would make my life a
nightmare if I didn't find her. But also, and
you have to promise to keep this a secret, I
was sort of growing a little fond of the old
girl. With her scaly skin, spikes, and distant
yellow eyes — she was hard not to love.

The windows in the classroom were
closed, so I knew that she was still in there.
When the bell rang for lunch, I hung outside
the door, peeking in through its window.

Unlike last night, Frankie and Ashley stuck around to help, even though there was no chance they'd get a free pizza out of it.

"She was definitely in the box when class started," I said. "She's got to be in there somewhere."

I peeked through the window again. Miss Adolf was seated at her desk, eating a sandwich and grading papers. My presentation was in the small rubbish bin by her feet. It was such a small rubbish bin that she had had to rip up my project several times to fit it in.

"Man, her sandwich is nauseating," Frankie said. "I can smell it from here."

I sniffed. "Pickled herring and sauerkraut. I think I'm developing super-smelling powers." I glared again at Miss Adolf, trying to send her a telepathic message to get up, stretch her legs, walk around, do something! "Will she stay in this room forever?" I asked in frustration.

"Impossible," Ashley said. "If she doesn't get up soon, she'll get deep vein thrombosis, and maybe even—"

"Trench foot?" I said.

"Oh Hank, you were listening! That's so sweet!"

"Look!" I said, and pointed. "Katherine's in Miss Adolf's bag!"

"I don't see it," Frankie said. "Oh wait, now I see it. There's a tail sticking out. Errgggh."

"We need to get her before Adolf does," I said. "If only we can get her out of that room..."

Something clicked in my brain.

CHAPTER TWENTY-ONE

It all seemed so simple and easy in my brain. But when I tried to translate what was in my brain into reality, it took a lot of paper, time and an entire Prussian army of little rubbers that I had thrown into my book bag this morning.

All three of us sat huddled on the floor in front of some lockers outside Miss Adolf's classroom. I had laid out three sheets of paper, on which I had drawn a scale map of the hallway and the classroom.

"OK," I said. "I'll go over it once more.

Try to listen this time, Frankie."

Frankie sighed.

"All right, it's really simple. First, we'll
synchronize our watches. And then, at
precisely 12:04, Frankie, you move into
position Bravo." I used a ruler to slide a
rubber labelled "F" to the Bravo spot on
the map – G4, if you're going by the grid.
"You stay put at G4 and keep watch of your
north-by-northeast vector."

"Huh?"

"Then, at 12:06, Ashley, you move
into position Delta." I slid her "A" rubber
accordingly. "Now make a note, this is
not your primary position. This is your
secondary position. You must not, under any
circumstances, make your way to position
Epsilon until 12:09, or unless I give the OK,
or unless we have to fall back to plan B,
at which point we'll rendezvous at position
Omega. Got it?"

"No!"

"And then, at exactly 12:07, I will deploy
the AI drone — Frankie, did you procure the
AI drone?"

"That's a negatory, chief."

"Frankie!" I sighed and rubbed my face all
over.

"Why don't I just go in and distract Miss
Adolf?" Ashley said. "And you run in and
grab Katherine."

"That sounds too complex," I said.
"Frankie?"

"I'm going with Ashley on this one.
Obviously."

"OK, I'm hungry, so let's just do it,"
Ashley said.

"Wait—" I yelled after Ashley, but she'd
already gone into the classroom. I moved a
few paces closer to the door and pressed
myself against the lockers, trying to blend
into the environment.

"Miss Adolf!" I heard Ashley yell. "Come
quick! Some girls are using multiple sheets

of loo roll in the toilets!"

"Two sheets, maximum!" Miss Adolf barked. "That's the rule. Lead the way, Miss Wong."

I really did feel myself start to blend into the lockers as Ashley and Adolf – fencing sword pressed against her shoulder – marched out of the class and strode right past me.

"Frankie, take up position Bravo and watch my flank," I whispered, before slipping inside.

CHAPTER TWENTY-TWO

I'd never been in my classroom all
alone before. It was kind of spooky. And
exhilarating. So many bad ideas came
streaming through my brain. Find Adolf's
grade book and change all my marks. Find
the Teacher's Edition textbook and become
a school legend. Set the clock ahead by
three hours. Put pizza grease on McKelty's
seat. Open all the windows and finally let
some fresh air into this drab and oppressive
torture factory!

No, Zipper Man, no. Don't open the

windows. *Katherine will climb out. Get Katherine.*

I sneaked over to the desk, moving in the shadows, and snatched Miss Adolf's messenger bag.

"Hey girl," I said opening it up.

But there was nothing alive in there. At least nothing I could see. Steeling all my courage, I reached my hand into the opening and riffled through Adolf's assorted sundries, feeling three sticks of old gum, a bottle of pills, a tube of lipstick, a knot of tights, and some sort of mass that I can only describe as "squishy".

"Hurry, Hank," Frankie whispered from position Bravo.

"I need just a few more seconds."

Then I saw her. Katherine was by the window. And the window was open! It was just open an inch, but the latch was undone, and all that was separating Katherine from Splat City three flights down was her nudging the window with her beak.

"There she is!"

"Adolf's coming, Hank. Wrap it up and fall back to position Epsilon!"

"I like the lingo, Frankie."

"Fall back to position Epsilon, Hank. Fall back now!"

"Stall her," I replied as I tiptoed towards Katherine, "OK Katherine, don't do anything stupid. You have so much to live for. Come with Uncle Hank..."

"She's coming, Hank! Abort! Abort!"

My hand hovered just above Katherine's cool, scaly skin, and I heard Frankie begin moaning and whimpering.

"Why are you lying on the floor in front of my classroom like a stray puppy, Frankie?" Miss Adolf asked.

"Oh, Miss, I'm so sick. My stomach. Take me to the school nurse."

"Miss Wong, take this malingerer to the nurse's office."

"But it looks pretty bad," Ashley said.

"Help me, Miss Adolf," Frankie wailed. "Argggh, it burns!"

"Now, Miss Wong. And if I find out you're up to something..."

Suddenly, I could feel Miss Adolf's presence in the classroom. I had two options: save myself, or save the lizard.

In case you don't remember the beginning of this book, I chose option one, and dived under Miss Adolf's desk ... also known as position Dead Meat.

CHAPTER
TWENTY-THREE

So, here we are again. And I'm still not invisible.

In case you're like me and you've got a short attention span, I'll re-set the scene. I am flat on my stomach, underneath Miss Adolf's desk. Miss Adolf has kicked off her shoes. Her feet are a hair's breadth from my nose, and, from the smell of them, they may have already contracted a raging case of trench foot. They surely live in a world that is terribly cold and damp. So while Miss Adolf is grading papers with her evil red pen up above, I'm down here and Katherine is on the window ledge, one mental and physical leap away from an untimely death. And to make matters worse, I feel a sneeze coming on. My face is starting to scrunch up. It's inevitable.

I had to face the facts. I can't eat metal. I can't sniff fear. And I can't make myself invisible. I can't even blend in!

No matter what I do, I end up in a mad situation. That's my only superpower. But you know what? That's not a bad one to have.

Because who wants to go their whole lives being invisible? Who wants to spend every day afraid of being noticed? Not me. I'm the bird with bright yellow feathers. I belong to the sacred order of anti-blenders. We're the real heroes in this world. Most of the time we get eaten, sure, but sometimes ... sometimes we're the ones who stand tall, who lead the brigade over the hill to victory, who change the world, who ...

... sneeze at exactly the wrong time.

But I was thinking fast. As I felt the sneeze rushing through my body, I took out my wallet and chucked it across the room to distract her. It clanked off a desk just as I smothered most of the sneeze somewhere in my neck. It worked, all right. But I did get clobbered when Adolf startled and kicked out. Trench foot right to the nose.

"What was that?" she said and sprang to her feet, raising her sword and sniffing the air. "Who's there? I know there's someone here. I can smell you, so just come out."

I watched her feet. Her very gross feet. She sneaked around the side of the desk and then pounced with a leap to the side. When her feet left the ground, I scurried out from under the desk and hid behind the other side of it, back pressed to the metal. She sniffed again.

Just then someone poked their nose through the door.

"State your business," Miss Adolf said.

"Ah, Miss Adolf." I recognized the voice. It was the school caretaker. He was a nice guy. Fond of cats. "Sorry to disturb someone as senior as you, but there's been an incident in the toilets."

"Oh?"

"Yes, with one of the cleaning staff and ... something about a sword."

"Really, how very odd." I saw Adolf hide the sword behind her back.

"She's very upset. And with your sense of authority and deep womanly compassion, well, I wondered if you could help me calm her down?"

"Surely it was just a hallucination, perhaps from those ghastly cleaning products," Miss Adolf said, and slid the sword out of sight right next to me. It was so sharp that it cut off three of my hairs. "Perhaps I might be able to talk some sense into the woman," she said, then jammed her smelly feet back into her shoes and clicked away into the hallway. The door closed.

"I'm alive," I whispered, and fist-pumped.

I sprang to my feet and turned to the window.

I didn't see anything at first. No need to panic, Katherine was probably just camouflaged. But then, as I got closer, I still didn't see anything, not even when I felt the day's cool breeze blowing through the wide-open window.

One thing that had absolutely not flown out of the open window? Locusts. I looked back at Miss Adolf's desk, where three giant, gross insects circled above her stinky sandwich. Someone, and I'm not saying it was me, must have forgotten to

take the plastic tub out of the classroom,
and also left it a tad bit open. Just enough
for them to learn that if they pushed,
they'd be free.

"Well, brain," I said as I bolted from
the class into the hallway, "we're officially
dead."

CHAPTER TWENTY-FOUR

Two days later, Emily was cleared for
release by her doctors. She was supposed to
come home the day after her surgery, but
they had to stay an extra day so Mum and
Dad's injuries could heal.

I used those two days searching the
classroom high and low for Katherine. I also
searched far beneath the windows, down
on the playground blacktop, for any grisly
stains. I found nothing – except for locusts.
The school was lousy with them. Those
things breed like you wouldn't believe. It

got so bad that a news team came over
and filed a very troubling story about the
sad state of London's schools. Then they
sprayed our school with a mist they said
wasn't toxic, but from everyone's red eyes,
you would have thought it was mustard gas.

When I wasn't at school, I spent all my
time trying to make a fresh lizard from stuff
around the house, just something to fool
Emily for long enough for me to find the
real Katherine. But I got kind of sidetracked
with the rubber cement. If you brush a coat
of it on your skin and it dries, it looks scaly.
So it was great fun to coat my arms with
the stuff and then rub off the scales into
little rubber cement balls, and store all the
little balls in a cup on my desk...

Like I said, sidetracked.

I had a close call yesterday when Emily
called on the video phone. It's a good job
I had printed out a picture of Katherine
for a "lost pet" flier, so when she called,

Katherine appeared to be hanging out on my bed in the background. Thank goodness lizards spend most of their time just sitting around and not moving.

The flier bought me some time, but it wouldn't last. So I stopped trying to concoct a replacement lizard out of spare parts, and started trying to figure out a way to buy a plane ticket to Tegucigalpa, Honduras, without any major credit cards.

I had just finished entering the numbers of my go-kart "junior driver" licence into the airline website when I heard keys jangling outside the front door.

I froze like a trapped animal, my eyes darting around. The only way out was the window. And the only lizard in the flat was the one I'd printed out. As quickly and silently as possible, I sprinted to the lizard printout, wrote "Gone fishing" on the back, rubber-cemented it to the door, and dived under my bed. I got as still as possible, concentrating, praying that for once in my life I could become invisible.

Yes, I know what I said about being the heroic anti-blender. But that was two days ago. When I find Katherine, I'll stick a feather in my cap. But until then, I don't want Emily to eat me alive. Come forth hidden superpower, don't fail me now!

"Come on, love," my dad was saying. "Why don't you go and lie down?"

"That would be lovely, Stan," Mum said. "My head is killing me."

"I was talking to Emily."

"I want some ice cream," Emily croaked.

I heard the freezer open. "It's all gone," Mum said.

"All of it?" Dad said.

"Very supportive, Hank," Mum muttered to herself, and with my mind's eye I could see her shaking her head. "Well, let's run you a nice bath instead."

"Ooh, that'd be nice."

"I was talking to Emily."

The freezer shut, and I heard Emily's little feet traipsing down the hallway. For a moment I thought she paused at my door, but then she threw open the door to her own bedroom.

"Come, my sweet," she croaked with a sigh. "Where's my sweet girl? Are you in here? Where are you?" Then her croaking grew louder and more reptilian. "Hank! Where are you, Katherine? Mum! Hank lost Katherine! Mum!"

CHAPTER TWENTY-FIVE

I didn't move a muscle when Emily burst into my room croaking for blood. She didn't see me, though. I guess it was hard for her to see through all the tears.

Mum and Dad didn't see me either. They didn't even look in, just saw my note about going fishing. What? It always works in cartoons.

Mum sighed. "I don't have the strength to handle whatever Hank's up to," she said. "My head is killing me. You'll do it, won't you, love?"

"Me?" Dad said. "I can't even bend over."

"But I've got head trauma."

"But I'm also the one who has to call Miss Adolf back about whatever Hank's done this time. Why do I have to talk to that woman?"

"Because she called your mobile," Mum said.

"But—"

"Stan, I've had enough trouble helping Emily through this complex time. I'm going to run a bath."

"But I'm the one in the back brace!"

"And I'm the one who had her tonsils out," Emily croaked. "I'm the one with no ice cream. I'm the one with no lizard. If you both don't help me find Katherine right now, then I'm going to—"

"OK, OK," Mum and Dad sighed.

Once I had heard the three of them start tearing Emily's room apart in search of yellow eyes, I slithered out of the flat, sent an SOS and met up with my mates at the

Spicy Salami. We had a lot of strategy to plan. Papa Pete was wiping the table where Frankie and Ashley met up with me.

Man, I felt wretched. "Emily's never going to forgive me," I said. "If only I'd just grabbed that lizard when I'd had the chance. It's just like World War I."

"Huh?" Frankie said.

"Frankie, lemme see your wallet." I implored. "Do you have, like, a twenty? Maybe I can get another lizard. They can't cost more than twenty quid, can they? They all look the same, don't they?"

"Not to Emily, they don't," Ashley said.

"It's true that there'll never be another Katherine." I hung my head. "But maybe, with an old photo of her, I can find one that looks exactly like her."

"Not with my twenty."

Papa Pete put his big hands on my shoulders. "Hank, there's only one way this time."

131

"Hypnotize Emily into believing she never had a lizard?" I felt everyone looking at me. I even felt myself looking at me. This was really crumby. "Tell her the truth. But I hate the truth!"

"You'll be all right," Frankie said. "We'll come with you, and take up position Bravo."

"Thanks guys, but I think this has to be a solo mission."

And as I got up, I accidentally bumped the table with both knees, sending no less than three plates shattering to the cold hard floor. "I hate tables too."

I had a long walk back. You know how three weeks can vanish in the blink of an eye? Well, this ten-minute walk lasted a century. I had to tell Emily that I had lost her best friend. I know that Katherine's just a lizard, but friends are friends, and Katherine's really not so bad. For a moment there, we were almost bonding.

I stopped before the door to my flat. The hundred-year walk was over. On the other side of the door was the truth. And the truth was that I was a major screw-up. I shook myself all over, took a deep breath and let out my getting-down-to-business shriek. Miss DeLillo pounded her ceiling beneath me with her broomstick. I stamped my feet loudly in response. "Not now, not now!"

I opened the door and walked in with my eyes closed. I opened an eye. Everyone was sitting on the sofa, huddled around something. Seeing nothing life threatening, I opened the other eye. On the coffee table, in front of the sofa, I saw the shredded remains of my pizza-box presentation.

"Well, Hank," Dad said with folded arms. "What have you got to say for yourself?"

"Look, I know I messed up my history project. I should have tried harder and all, but there's something I have to say first. Emily, I lost Katherine. I took her to school.

I wanted to use her in my project. She's such a cool animal, and I wanted to show everyone that, but Miss ... but I lost her. I lost her for ever and it's all my fault. I'll do anything to make it up to you."

From her blankets on the sofa, Emily looked at me blankly. I could read nothing on her face. This was the worst. She was too hurt to do anything. But behind those beady, unmoving eyes of hers, I knew she was plotting her sweet revenge.

"I'll do anything," I said.

"Anything?" she croaked.

"Anything, Emily. I promise. I'll clean your room. I'll get you a real, human friend. I'll even eat locusts."

"So basically, you'll be my slave?"

I felt my life force draining out of my ear. But there was nothing left for me to do but agree to it. "I will." Seeing the sadistic gleam in her eye, I added hurriedly, "For a week."

"Hmmm. What do you think, Katherine?"

"Katherine?"

Camouflaged in Emily's greyish blanket, I now saw a yellow eye looking blankly at me.

"While you were out fishing, Hank," Dad said, "I went to see your teacher at school. She showed me these ripped-up pizza boxes, and at first I had no idea why your teacher wanted to show me all this rubbish. But it turned out rubbish was also your history project. Well done, kiddo."

"But it really looked cool before Miss—"

"Miss Adolf also told me," my dad went on, "that you claimed there was a live lizard inside those pizza boxes. She didn't believe you of course. But then this afternoon, while she was grading your paper, she happened to find a live lizard behind a filing cabinet. What do you have to say for yourself?"

"That you guys should be proud of me. I didn't lie to my teacher."

"I think you owe your sister an apology," Mum said.

"I already gave her one."

"I accept your apology, Hank."

"Great! That's great, Em. So since Katherine's back and you're not angry at me anymore, that means that we're—"

"Slaves will report for duty at 7 a.m."

CHAPTER TWENTY-SIX

Well, everything's back to normal. As normal as it can be when you're someone's slave. Katherine didn't have any emotional scars from her time in my classroom, and Emily is back to her usual annoying self. She is a cruel, croaky taskmaster. It helps that she can't talk much while her throat is healing, but resourceful Emily has found a way around that.

Yes, that's right. Whenever Emily rings her bell, I have to come running.

"Coming! Do you feel calm and

supported?"

"I need more ice cream."

"At once, Emily."

"And more *Acrididae* for Katherine."

"Ackriwhat?"

"Bugs."

If I don't answer fast enough, she keeps ringing that blasted bell.

"At once, master."

I know, I know. It's humiliating. But I've been working on my superpowers. I've been practising hypnosis. If I get really good at it, maybe I'll be able to make Emily forget that I promised to eat locusts.

And if not, then, hey, at least locusts have protein. It's got to be better than eating metal, right?

Oh, who am I kidding? You win, Emily. You win, and I lose.

My life is a nightmare!!!!!!!!!!!!

THE COLOSSAL
CAMERA CALAMITY

Hank hates school photos. No matter what he
does, he always ends up looking like he's just
seen Miss Adolf dancing. Bleurgh! This year,
he's determined to get it right. Unfortunately,
school bully Nick McKelty has other ideas...

THE COW POO
TREASURE HUNT

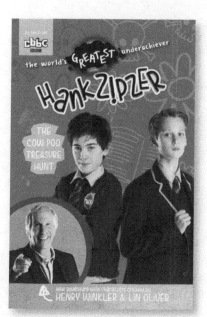

At Westbrook Academy, the school camping trips are legendary for all the wrong reasons. This year Hank is teamed up with his nemesis, McKelty. A leaky tent, a treasure hunt in a field of cowpats and Nick McKelty – can life get any worse?!

THE BALLOT BOX BRAWL

A school council seat is up for grabs, and Nick McKelty and Emily Zipzer are campaigning to get it. Hank's plan to stop them from getting power is to run for the position himself, and the election gets ugly fast. What won't they do for votes?